The Elements

By Patsy Stanley

ISBN 978-0-9997453-6-6
ISBN 978-0-9997453-5-9

LCCN 2018908829

The branch of Philosophy dealing with Spiritual Substances is called Occult Pneumatology…

In the End, You Must Trust the Dark and Seek the Light….

All of the cloaks/bodies we have donned so we could manifest here, those bodies, regardless of their vibration, are governed by universal hierarchies of Ancients who organize, promote, and keep us on our path of character development each lifetime. And so it is, that different Ancient groups have different genetic birthrights. A part of who we are, forever remains in the Earth, and in the Stones, and in the Wind when we leave Earth, giving back to it, the cloaks we wore while we were here.

Every Master that is your teacher is a strand of your Cosmic DNA.

The Elemental Mysteries:

The Elemetal energies are reflected and active through the feminine nature in hue-mans. The elemental energies and the feminine nature are one and the same throughout existence. In this book we will address the feminine nature and the higher thinking about the elements.
This book is a birth story about the Elements and the Creation Story of the Atom...it is a book about the larger universal nature of women

According to Science, tt all began out there...

Enstein's theory of general relativity stated that the space-time around earth was not only warped but twisted by the planet's rotation.

Essentially, his theory determined that the laws of physics are the same for all non-accelerating observers and that the speed of light in a vacuum is the same no matter the speed an observer travels at. That is to say that both space and time were interwoven into a single continuum called space-time. His equations further showed that massive objects caused a distortion in the space-time continuum.

This would be like placing a large object in the middle of a trampoline. The weight of the object presses in to the fabric creating a dimple. A marble rolling around the edge would spiral inward toward the object. It is being pulled in very much the same way that the gravity of a planet pulls at objects in space.

Physics and Cosmology have developed a theoretical, scientific Creation story for the atom. This story tells us that everything in the world is made of atoms, and how atoms came to be. Science believes that the path to enlightenment lies in understanding the death of stars, that the stories of the galaxies and stars are our
1
stories; that to understand the life process of a star is to understand our own history.
Scientists believe that the first elements were forged in the galaxy during the Big Bang, almost fourteen billion years ago, and that the catastrophic death of a star brings new life to all parts of the universe, and that every piece of us was forged in the furnaces of a dying star.

The universe and everything in it is made of atoms. Every atom we are made of was created out there in the universe. Where we come from is where the elements came from.

Here's the process:

Stars are indeed born from nebulae and consist mostly of hydrogen and helium gas. Surface temperatures range from 2000C to above 30,000C and the corresponding colors from red to blue white. The brightest stars have masses 100 times that of the Sun and emit as much light as millions of Suns. They live for less than a million years before exploding as supernovae. The faintest stars are the red dwarfs, less than one-thousand the brightness of the Sun.

A star is "born" in a stellar nursery called a nebula which is a cloud of gas (hydrogen) and dust in space. A star's life cycle is determined by its mass or size. The larger the mass, the shorter the life cycle. Over time, the hydrogen gas in the nebula is pulled together by gravity and begins to spin. As the gas spins faster it heats up, eventually reaching temperatures of 15,000,000 degrees. It is at this stage that nuclear fusion occurs in the core of the cloud. The cloud will glow brightly, contract slightly, then become stable. It is now considered a main sequence star and will shine for billions of years. Our sun is in this stage.

Each star burns for eons of time, until their need for fuel causes them to become a red giant. They expand until they become red giants and finally explode. In that instant after the explosion, sub atomic particles acquire mass for the first time. The particles start as quarks which is an elementary particle and a very basic part of matter. Quarks combine to form composite particles called hadrons, the most stable of which are protons and neutrons and are the components of atomic nuclei.

When a star glows, hydrogen is converted into helium by nuclear fusion. When the hydrogen starts to run out and the star isn't generating heat through nuclear the fusion, the core becomes unstable and contracts. The outer shell of the star begins to expand. It cools as it expands and glows red. It has entered the red giant phase.

The red glow is because the star is cooler than it was in the main sequence stage, and is a giant because the outer shell, which is hydrogen, has expanded. Helium now fuses into carbon in the core of the red giant.

From that point on, the evolutionary cycle of a star is determined by its size. A low mass star, like our Sun, collapses again after the helium has fused into carbon. As it collapses, the layers of the star are expelled, and a planetary nebula is formed. The core remains as a white dwarf, and eventually cools to become a black dwarf.

In a high mass star, the evolution is the same until it reaches the red giant phase. Core temperatures increase as carbon atoms are formed from the fusion of the helium atoms. As the temperature increases, gravity pulls the carbon atoms together and more fusion processes continue forming oxygen, nitrogen and eventually iron.
Massive stars go through supernova explosions. If the remnant of the explosion is 1.5 up to 3 times the mass of our sun, then it becomes a neutron star. If it is greater than 3 times the mass of our sun, the evolution is different. The force of gravity overcomes the nuclear forces which keep protons and neutrons from combining. The core is swallowed by its own gravity and becomes a black hole. A black hole attracts any matter and energies that comes near it.

Fusion stops when the core contains only iron. Iron is the most stable and compact of all elements available in the star, and takes more energy to break up than any other element. That is to say that to create heavier elements through the fusing of iron would require an input of energy rather than release. At this point, there is no energy being radiated from the core; the star begins its final phase of gravitational collapse. The core temperatures rise to well over 10 million degrees Kelvin, initiating the proton chain reaction and allowing hydrogen to fuse, first to deuterium and then to helium, as the iron atoms are crushed together.

The force between the nuclei overcomes the force of gravity causing the core to recoil out of the heart of the star in a shock wave. We see this shock wave as a supernova explosion.

The material in the star's outer layers are heated from the shock, and fuse to form new elements and radioactive isotopes. Most common elements, like carbon and nitrogen, are created in the core of most stars, fused from lighter elements like hydrogen and helium. Three helium atoms fuse together to make carbon, element #6, releasing energy in this process.

All the other elements can be made from hydrogen, which has one proton and one electron in each atom. Helium is the second simplest element with two protons and two electrons per atom. This basic building material for everything is put in place in the few seconds after the dying star explodes.

The star continues to go through a series of heating and cooling events, dying in stages, enabling the organizing of more and different elements into their complexity. This complexity is achieved by adding more and more protons and neutrons to each atom.

Hydrogen is the simplest element. All stars burn hydrogen. When they run out of it, they begin to die. The star becomes hotter and explodes, expanding into a huge size that it cannot maintain. It starts to cool and becomes a red giant, a star dying in stages.

It is in these stages that the elements are formed.

In stage one, it runs out of hydrogen.

In stage two, helium nuclei fuse together, forming carbon and oxygen in the heart of the dying star.

In stage three, carbon fuses with aluminum, magnesium, sodium, and neon.

Everything is made of the same basic ingredients, carbon and calcium, including the organic molecules in our body.

Elements are rarely formed by themselves. They are combined forms. Elements by themselves are extremely reactive. It is this reactivity that enables the elements to combine with one another to make new substances. That makes for an endless variety on earth, including us.

Each stage is hotter than the last, until it becomes almost all iron, and the fusion process stops. During the implosion, the first twenty-six elements are formed naturally.

There are sixty elements heavier than iron that occur naturally, and they are only forged in rare conditions that last about one minute once every hundred years. The stars producing these rare conditions have to be at least nine times the size of our sun. The star has to be that big to be hot enough to create by fusion, the rarer sixty elements such as platinum and gold.

Those rare elements developed once every hundred years, align with the character development of our Higher Nature, which vibrates faster, while the rest of the Elements resonate with the development of our lower nature, which vibrates slower. The faster or higher energies of those sixty Elements are fed to us through the chakras that revolve around our heads and bodies.

A supernova is the explosive reaction of a high mass star, and in their final death throes they shoot out the Elements. One of the things those Elements do is to create a nebula, a birth nursery for more stars to be born in. This is the mirroring process for the Feminine Nature, or, the Nature of Matter and how it manifests in humanity and everywhere else.

Because a super nova event occurs about once every hundred years, the sixty Elements created by them in their final stage of death are found in limited amounts on Earth.

The assembly process for building the elements is called nuclear fusion. That process can only happen in the biggest of stars. We contain the entire history of the universe. Our beginnings go far past the dawn of humanity, clear back to the beginnings of the universe. We are made of the universe. We were forged in the stars…

The rich and varied chemistry of Earth extends far out into space. The Moon is rich in helium, silver, and water. Mars is rich in iron. Venus is rich in sulfur. Each of these Elements are aligned with certain aspects of the character development of themselves, Earth, and all that exists on Earth. These are cosmic covenants made between living beings, supervised by planetary Regents and Masters.

Encoded in the star light that bathes planet Earth are the keys to understanding what the universe is made of, and the understanding of how each chemical element is formed. We are bathed in this information all the time, and a percentage of the humans on Earth focus on and pursue these understandings.

Heated elements give off light. Each set of elements gives off its own particular set of colors. Sodium is yellow. Copper is blue. Potassium is lilac. Each Element has its own characteristic color. These colors tell us what Elements the stars are made of. Each star emits and absorbs the same colors.

Using color tools, scientists have found that there are the same ninety two elements in the universe, and the same amount on Earth.

Carbon 12 was chosen in early 1960's to measure mass, not structure. It was chosen because of its coherence to Avogadro's Principle, its stability and abundance, and basically to stop everybody from fighting. Carbon - 12 also more accurately defines as mass for hydrogen and it is unbound in its ground state.
Carbon contains 6 protons, 6 electrons, and 6 neutrons. This is what we are made of. This internal abundance is due to the triple alpha process by which it is created in Stars. Carbon 12 atoms are Star material, and they are the standard scientists use to measure all other atomic structures.

Human beings are made of star material, and so is everything else. That means that we, as human beings, are fed energy from the universe, the galaxies, the stars, the moons and planets through the chakra systems. The energies we are made of, was forged in the stars millions of years ago. We are responsible for not only our personal combination of these energies, but for how we use the Earth's energies, and for our galactic, universal, and cosmic energies and relationships.

We all are truly a part of all that is, and equally share in the immense opportunities and responsibilities our universe offers us to expand and understand more of life.

From modern day science, back to the cave people, the wonder of Creation has been interpreted through story and song, creating an extraordinary and very diverse amount of information about how Creation works to be fought over, pondered, and believed - or not. All the stories contain the same basic themes of Motion, Matter, and its applicable Holiness…

Earth's Sacred Elemental Systems

The associations formed by the /colors and elements/the eternal mother and father/the electron and proton/ in each atom provide us with the world we live in.

It is through their interaction and the child, or neutron's balancing of their combined energies, that our world is constantly created, providing us with a future.

The hierarchies that govern their associations provide us with the time, weight, space and measure that form our reality.

Auriel or Uriel-is the Regent of the Element of Earth.
San dal phon or Malkuth, The living Sphere of Earth, and Auriel, have an interlinked relationship, each being a Regent of a dense aspect of force…

When humankind is able to maintain all of the Elements in Balance, they Overcome, and thus, shield themselves from the dominance and control of their lower Nature…….

There is an elemental kingdom surrounding each chakra of each piece of manifested Matter, from the planet itself down to the tiniest insect; linking All to the universe.

Esoteric teachings tell us that Hue-man beings have at least seven chakras. Each one of those chakras is ringed by an Elemental kingdom whose borders mirror the universal Ring Pass Not. Each kingdom is made up of our issues and the fixes for that issue; those issues having been set in place (by us and others/Masters/Guides/Angelic orders/etc.) to forward our character development. Each kingdom surrounding each chakra maintains a specific kind of magic that belongs to humans/plants/animals/everything; magic we earned through lessons learned in our past lives. Every elemental kingdom is a magic ring bordering plant, mineral, and animal hierarchies, as well as Guides, Beings, and Others. It is out of these spiritual, sacred Kingdoms that our fairy tales, folk lore, and magic proceed.

The Upanishads describe the most ancient Hindu spiritual chakra system; the three major Elements and four Minor Elements that convert into human spiritual values.

1. The Adi –electric-positive- works with the proton-Father
2. The anapadaka-negative and magnetic-works with the electron-Mother
3. The neutron-works with the Akashic or Ether element- it is the home of Nirvana, of aha's and realizations. The Child.

Out of the three major elements proceed the four minor elements. The four minor elements are:

1. Fire
2. Air
3. Earth
4. Water

These Minor Elements and their symbols are referred to in all major religious texts, as well as in astrology and tarot, and in countless other ways.
They are referred to in chemistry as: CHON
   ¬ Earth- carbon
   ¬ Water- hydrogen
   ¬ Air- oxygen
   ¬ Fire- nitrogen
In psychology, these elements serve as the energies of experience and expression of our human experiences. The Earth and Water

C/H provide experiencing. The Air and Fire O/N provide the expression of those experiences.

The three Major elements are the pure Essence of Form, of Matter. Their existence provides creation with the balance needed in the universe. It is through them that energy transmission is made possible.

The four lower elements provide the Creation we live in with its Seasons and much more.

- ¬ The Earth Element being Winter
- ¬ The Water Element being Spring
- ¬ The Air Element being Fall
- ¬ The Fire Element being Summer

Each of the bodies of the self, the physical, mental, astral, and soul, have a primary association with each one of the four lower Elements and its accompanying season.

- ¬ The physical body is associated with the Earth Element and the season Winter.
- ¬ The astral/emotional body is associated with the Water Element and the season Spring.
- ¬ The Mental body is associated with the Air Element and the season Fall.
- ¬ The soul/lower causal body is associated with the Fire Element and the season Summer.

The Beings that govern the Elemental energies are pure and sacred. They are very serious Beings. They don't have to teach any human being or let anyone learn about them. You have to earn that right. That right is anchored in your character development. You have to become a person with enough character development to gain their approval because character development is under their domain.

The way human beings are trained to use the Electron or Feminine Force in their life, is provided to them by their mother, through their relationship with her. A human being's relationship with their mother determines the patterns for how Life is received. Mother provides the patterns for how a person will connect to Life. How a person forms their relationships, and how strong the relationship will be, and how long it will last, those patterns are given through the mother. Anything a human being is attracted to, comes from the magnetic, attracting mother principle.

People connect to the different parts of themselves, to the physical, astral, mental and soul bodies, using the same connective patterns their mother used to connect to her bodies. A person will follow that same pattern until the patterning changes, or they change it deliberately through examining their internal motives and ways of being. Taking one's own inventory and changing it is not always easy, but it can be a wondrous journey that will set one free. And many times, the mother in us yearns for us to be free.

The Elemental Mysteries

One must earn the right through reverence for, and respect of, the taking on of the responsibilities attached to each aspect of the Elements before one can access the deeper attributes and understandings that are developed through the Kingdoms.

The Elements and how they work are The Great Mysteries. They are under the safekeeping of the Elemental Kingdoms and it is through the development of one's character that we earn the right to be taught by the Elemental hierarchies about connection and how it all works. The light and dark combine to develop desirable character traits as well as undesirable traits. All are made of both, but their driver is always towards goodness/the Highest Good of All.

The nucleus in each atom of everything is surrounded by an electron cloud. This cloud symbolizes the Great Mystery that is contained in each atom of everything. The Mystery Schools are higher mental plane respondents to the electron cloud. They are the keepers and assist in the protection of Matter and its Mysteries both up and down the energy planes.
All monasteries, cloisters, abbys, religious retreats, are part of the protection and service programs existing in our conscious physical world for the upkeep of the Great Mysteries.

The Elemental hierarchies are much more responsible than human beings are. They do not understand what we as human beings do to ourselves, nor do they like it. They recognize our intentions immediately, whether we are trying to hide them or not.

When approaching any Elemental Beings, make yourself as clean as you possibly can. Drink water and eat sparingly of clean, live food for as long as you can before you approach them.

They don't like profanity or disrespect, and they won't put up with chattering or doing anything fast. Be careful to not wear makeup or perfumes or rings and symbols. Those things might mean something very different to you than they do to them. And it might not be positive.

The Elemental Beings have to be approached with great respect and gravity. Move slowly, and think respectfully. No jokes or smart alec stuff. They don't care how much you think you know.

However you approach them, they are probably going to tell you no to entering their kingdoms. They are very serious, and won't be rushed into anything.
They may or may not answer your questions. They don't have to. You have to do the work of connecting to them. That means getting more responsible for what you were sent here for. They don't have to do anything.

Your intention is seen by them, and will be responded to appropriately and immediately.

They do not have what we call manners. They give the truth to you without caring how you feel or think about it.

The Elemental Kingdoms hold the access to the Mysteries of Life itself. They protect the Mysteries from harm by keeping them secret so they can't be used by humans to harm other life forms.

There are permanent responsibilities that go with gaining Elemental awareness, for it is through the Elements that all form is made possible; that all Matter materializes. The more responsible we are, the slower and more deliberate we become. Responsibilities slow us down. They are made of Matter. They are permanent commitments of our time and energy.

It is through the elemental energies that the higher abilities of humankind are able to manifest in a balanced, useful, and responsible, grounded manner.

One might say that there is a mini-Mystery school in every atom of our being.

The wonderful, magical and stern hierarchies that govern each of the Elements are a part of the Elemental Studies. The Elements, the electron in the atom, serves as the Force of attraction, contraction, and manifestation throughout all of creation.

Each of the chakras works with an Elemental Kingdom administered by a Spherical Kingdom, which is overseen by a Sisterhood that keeps form in place in that area.

Each sisterhood works with a Color Brotherhood. Together, they keep in balance the wave/motion/ particle/matter associated with each chakra and its attendant Elemental Kingdom.

The Elemental Guides provide connection to the Kingdoms for each part of Life so that it may manifest into Form.

Above the Brotherhoods and Sisterhoods, lie the higher Spiritual Hierarchies that govern them. The Regents of Planets and the Governors of Hierarchies and more reside here. The denial of access to the Kingdoms is under the protection of the Elemental Kingdoms and is what holds the planet and all manifestation of matter in place, including humanity. The Elemental Kingdoms are the birth place of the Word 'No".

In order to manifest onto this planet and live out a human life, we have to have gathered enough Matter to do so. This is where what we call "issues" come in. The Matter we are formed of is made of our issues from past lives and the current issues we came in with. Our issues are flavored with Earth's issues, too.

The "issues" we have are not accidents. We chose the combination of issues we have to further our character development. We have to have a purpose to be in this classroom of life. The "cloaks" we don when we manifest here are made of our issues. They are our "coats of many colors." Our issues give us purpose. They make it possible for us to stay here. If we are too "enlightened", we don't have enough Matter or issues to manifest or to stay here.

There are many factors involved in the choices of where we manifest and why, most of which we humans aren't consciously aware of. But we can deduce on a larger scale that those choices have to with our involution and evolutionary processes, and everything to do with our Karmic purpose. We have to keep growing and knowing. It is the Law that rules "All".

So, trust yourself and the ongoing processes in your life. In a larger way of thinking, they have purpose and dignity. You are at the right place and in the right time. Whether it is negative or Positive; trust the Universe and learn. You are who you are in the greater scheme of life; that is on purpose. We have an effect on the past, present, and future of all of our generations and all of life as it occurs in our reality. That is a big deal.

The Elemental hierarchies that protect and serve Matter are ascribed different functions and names in different cultures:

Here is a brief history of the Eastern Elements.

The Elemental Kingdoms are known as the "Deva" Kingdoms in Creation in the Eastern religions. The Vedic period, which ran from about 1500 BC to 500 BC, named the "Deva's" in the "Vedas". These texts are preserved in the mantras of the Four Vedas, a large body of four religious Hindu texts.

"Deva" is an ancient Sanskrit word meaning God. In Hindu and Buddhism, both non-Christian religions, "Deva" means a divine being or a God.
"Devas" are Radiant beings who serve as Guardians to the Elemental hierarchies.
"Devas" structure and keep in order, and oversee the functions of Nature. They maintain and protect the boundaries of each Elemental Kingdom.
"Devas" guard and protect whole areas of elemental beings and nature. They hold the core matrix or picture, steadfast and in keeping for the manifestation of Nature in a particular area.
The "Devas" of each area present to the people living in that part of Nature, pictures of what they are allowed to see of the Nature that lives there.

The "Devas" work with Elemental beings; those being the Nature spirits who are the servants of God, humans, and others dwelling within the planes of Matter, in service of the electron force.
There are seven left handed charged leptons in each atom; they generate a magnetic field as they rotate around the electron, radiating out in a full three hundred and sixty degrees. They

express the elements into form through the Elemental Kingdoms.

In the oldest of Pagan and other beliefs, these sacred hierarchies include nature spirits and all kinds of other beings such as gnomes, mermaids, salamanders, fairies, elves. They are the energy expressers and servers of the leptons that rotate around the electron; they serve as expressors of the forces of attraction, contraction, and manifestation in the universe, the glue that holds it all together. It is through the electron force that we learn how to manifest our highest creative potential.

A history of the electron.

Awareness of the Electron came when "The Enuma Elis", a text of Babylon Mythology, the 18th. – 16th. Century, B.C. named the Elements.

Empedocles 490 - 430 B.C. Defined the Electron in Atomic structure and assigned the four physical divisions to the Elements. He named them "Roots". Plato was the first to refer to them as Elements.

They were:
- Earth
- Water
- Air
- Fire

These four elements became what the known world or matter was composed of. He listed the four Elements that could be seen in the physical world. He said,

"To the Elements it came from,
Everything will return.
Our bodies to Earth,

Our blood to water,
Heat to Fire,
Earth to Air."

Plato 424-348 B.C. was a student of Socrates.

Aristotle 384-322 B.C. was a student of Plato.

Aristotle was a teacher of Alexander the Great.

Aristotle took the Greek theories Empedocles had propounded about the Elemental substances, changed their name from roots to elements, and put them into a linear construct that is still in use today.

He named the four elements Earth, Water, Air, and Fire and the unseen Element "the fifth Element, Ether. He assigned all of the unseen and the unknown world to the Ether Element.

Paracelcus.1493-1541 was a Swedish alchemist and physician who assigned symbols to the four elements.

- Symbolizing the fire element is the Salamander.
  Definition:
  A mythical animal having the power to endure fire
  without being harmed. In the theory of Paracelcus, this
  was a being inhabiting the fire element.

- Symbolizing the air element is the Sylph.
  Definition:
  An imaginary being that inhabits the air, a name given by
  Paracelsus to the elemental beings of the air, conceived
  by him as mortal but soulless. A slender, graceful
  woman.

- ¬ Symbolizing the water element is the Undine.
  Definition:
  Root: under a water wave. A fabled female water spirit who might receive a human soul by marrying a mortal.

- ¬ Symbolizing the earth element is the Gnome
  Definition:
  Root Word- To know. One of a fabled race of diminutive subterranean beings, guardians of mines, tunnels, quarries, etc.

Elemental beings were given life because of the Elemental Kingdom's work to create Matter from Devic Substance. "Devas" are natural channels for energy to pour through. From the King "Devas" to other "Devas", depending on evolutionary process of the specific Glen, to smaller groups, down to "Devas" of trees, flowers and grass, these Radiant Beings keep the Nature Hierarchies in order.

Euclid's Table of Elements was the first written work humans have a record of, that breaks the four classic Elements down into more Elemental divisions.

The excesses of the elemental energies are thrown off as color energies. Different Elements have different compositions; therefore each has different Elemental hierarchies.

- ¬ Fire Elementals reside on the soul planes.
- ¬ Air Elementals reside on the mental planes.
- ¬ Water Elementals reside on the astral plane.
- ¬ Earth Elementals reside on the physical planes of energy.

A nature spirit is a physical elemental that works with the earth element. Here are more:
- ¬ Leprechauns
- ¬ Gnomes

- o Gnomes are servers, and live under trees
  - o To draw gnomes and Earth elementals into your home, make a doll house for them in a corner. Give them something to swing on and walking canes. They will live there and go in and out of the levels of reality. Talk to them humbly and politely.
- ¬ Elves
- ¬ Fairies
- ¬ Trolls demand respect, are servers who do lots of work and hold the secrets of many things
  - o Trolls are big and ugly. They live under bridges or dams or overhanging cliffs.
- ¬ Brownies are small, delicate, astral in feeling, and are found in fields and in field mouse holes. They are afraid of denseness.
- ¬ Goblins are grotesque looking. They are nasty but can be useful. They live under tree trunks and under brush piles.

- ¬ Leprechauns are solitary cobblers who lived mostly in Ireland. Found only in clean areas, they were once in the physical, but left because of negativity.

The Water Element- H_2O

Mermaids live in salt water. Undines or Sprites live in fresh water, clear mountain streams, or under waterfalls. They work with the water element. They are big, like people. To bring this element and them into your home, use anything that works with water, such as water scenes or fountains.

The Air Element

Fairies come in a variety of shapes and sizes. They work with trees, flowers, blossoms. These little forms work with specific energies.

For example, one might work with one specific type of flower in a particular color. All Feathers are made by fairies. They control this. To bring them into your home, place chimes, forest scenes, and bells around.

The Fire Element
Salamanders live and dance at the tip of flames. You can see a salamander in fires. Their eyes are the embers. To bring them into your home, get an empty match box and place it near a picture of fire.

You can create a room for nature spirits. Just place pictures on the four walls, corresponding to the directions, then add other things to go with the pictures. For special feeling or good effect, put or make special scenes in corners or on walls.

Remember, dreams are real. Don't give up on them. Your focus and being specific are important.

Ongoing Character Development:
When working consciously and deliberately with the Elements, the following benefits occur:

- ¬ The Elements make possible free will choice. They provide one with the freedom to choose.
- ¬ One will expand their conscious awareness of themselves and the universe.
- ¬ One will gain greater control of one's personal energies.
- ¬ One will gain greater control of one's outer life.
- ¬ One will be able to understand more. One will feel more connected, better able to take care of themselves, feel more secure, and more grounded, and clearer about what's going on.

However, that is no guarantee that one will get what they want. But, one's identity will take root and grow.

- ¬ One will be more able to feed themselves. Typically, working with the Elements brings more responsibility.
- ¬ The expansion of conscious awareness of One's relationship to the creation all around one will increase.
- ¬ Awareness and acceptance of the rhythms of life and where one fits in, will increase.
- ¬ One will establish greater rapport between their bodies, allowing each of their energy vibrations to raise.
- ¬ The channels, through which the higher and lower natures blend and work together, will open more.

In working with the Elements, one becomes deliberate. This doesn't mean one won't make mistakes. It does mean that one will begin to take responsibility and clean up their mistakes when they find out about them.

Too many Elemental energies or an over balance to the magnetic, feminine nature manifests as:
- ¬ Catatonic states and all forms of withdrawal
- ¬ Lack of motion, depression

Too much negative in elemental energy patterns causes depression.

Anxiety is energy responding to depression.

Negative isolation and lack of speech. (expression)

The more you understand about the Elements and how they work with the Color energies, the more you understand about Creation. They work together. You can't have one without the other.

Writing, music, art, fairy tales, dreams, and prosperity, are all grounded in the Elements.
All access to Mastery of anything you can ever think of happens only through the Elemental Kingdoms.

ϖ   All shielding and forms of protection take place through the Elemental kingdoms.

ϖ   Jesus Christ was an Elemental Master.

ϖ   The book of Psalms in the Bible is a book of the Elements.

ϖ   The Old Testament in the Bible is a history of the proton, the angry male, and how separation works, the color energies.

ϖ   The New Testament in the Bible is a history of the electron, expressing the feminine power of connection in both its positive and negative aspects.

ϖ   The four Holy Living Creatures in the Cosmos are the symbolic reflections of the four Holy Creatures of Earth.

ϖ   If you are ritual poor, put more Elements in as building blocks for new rituals to emerge from.

The Four Classic Elements

In the Western world, the Elemental Kingdoms and their Radiant Beings are defined through the four Archangels and other angels. Modern western culture today teaches that the four minor elemental divisions are governed by four Arch Angels. The most powerful Angels are portrayed as male.

In earlier times and today in other cultures, there are often more Elements listed, governed by female masters, who in turn, are ruled by hierarchies of animal gods and goddesses.

The Beings that govern the Elemental energies are vast, ancient vortexes of energy. The Elemental energies are under their charge. All processes of Manifestation of Matter are under their supervision.

Whatever they have been labeled down through human history, these vortexes of energy are energy Masters who govern the processes of Involution and Evolution, keeping the balance in the great spiral of life. It is through these Master vortexes of energy that all of the plant, mineral, and animal kingdoms are worked with.

Sandalphon or Malkuth, The living Sphere of Earth, and Auricl, have an interlinked relationship, each being a regent of a dense aspect of the life force.

Sandalphon rules the structure of life forms within this planet, our evolution of consciousness, and of form upon this Earth, the people ruled over by "souls of fire", or the symbolic name for the consciousness of the Atom.

Ariel is the Regent of the Old Moon, and because of that, his/her power relates to inner earth and all potencies. The Old Moon is the one that preceded the one we have now. It is through Ariel that we feel the deepest respect for the owners of creation.

Auriel or Uriel, is also the Regent of the element of Earth. Ariel or Uriel, rules the basic forces of Earth itself. Ariel rules the seismic powers, and was connected with this planet before humans came here. Ariel Guided Earth's evolution before its form solidified. Ariel was here when Earth was passing through its fire and water stages. Ariel is the teacher of Enoch.

The Four Arch (Arc) Angels of the Elements

The Earth Element

The Arch Angel that governs the Earth Element is Auriel, or Uriel.

The Archangel that administers the energies of the Earth Element is Ariel, or (Uriel).
This Archangel is the Bearer of the Cross. Ariel helps us to become aware of God. It is through She/He that "the Lord makes his face to shine down upon thee and to be gracious to thee." This process takes place through the combination of the powers of the Great Cosmic Forces that pour through the chakras spinning around our heads.

The name Ariel means "Light of God". She/He brings Divinity into our hearts by the magic of love so that we feel God and become aware of Him/Her. Our souls grow as our love for God enlarges with the help of the Archangel Auriel. She/He is the Bearer of Divine Love, Knowledge and Truth; The Lord of Awe, who inspires in us a sense of the deepest respect for the wonders of creation.

He is the Archangel of Earth and its fertility.

Ariel administered the Great Deluge that we read about in the Bible, and helps as a server of greater powers.

It is through Ariel's agency that Fire, Water, and Air are permitted to esoterically do their work on the planet Earth.

It is through the Earth element that all three of the other basic Elements manifest their form, time, space, and weight.

The Earth element makes all elimination and assimilation possible.

During the Creation of Form:
The Earth Element Controls the Forces of Creation. In the Beginning, during the solidification process of form, light turned into magnetism, and radiance into gravity. This was a necessary Darkness, and went on for a long time before both were freed again.

The Earth Elements activities and functions are aligned with the masculine principle of Nature, thus giving Form its Motion.

The Earth Element Represents the Distillation of True Wisdom.

The Earth Element is responsible for creating both catastrophe's and peace on the physical plane.
The Earth Element is considered to be magnetic and feminine in its polarity. It is associated with wisdom, and gives form to the physical body. It works with the principle of fusion and implosion.
The invisible, magnetic grid surrounding the Earth holds it all together. That living grid and its emissaries protect us from outer influences that would harm us. They keep gravity in place. They hold us here so we can participate in the dual processes of involution and evolution.

In order for our consciousness to manifest on Earth, two initiations have to take place. Donning our physical form is the first initiation we receive on manifesting on Earth, and we return that physical form to the Earth upon leaving. This is the Law. This is the two part initiation we call birth and death that we go through in order to experience and express ourselves here on planet Earth.

Earth is the Bearer of Shields.

The Earth element governs the making and keeping of covenants. Covenant making is very poetic and employs the use of higher symbols. This is one of the reasons Elemental beings are repulsed by blasphemy.
The shield and the staff are the Earth Element's symbols, the shield being the device of protection on the lower planes of energy, and the staff being the symbol of stability on the higher planes of energy. The staff is also the device, the staff of the Magician for strength and the ability to gain that strength.

The Earth element teaches a reverence for the beauty of growth, a reverence and deep respect for the physical aspects of life. It opens the way for the energies of the higher abilities of humans to manifest and to stay balanced.
When working with Earth energies, one comes to learn each of the physical body's resources, what that resource is attached to on the energy planes, where it draws its strength from, and what the body connections are to other realms.
You begin to understand the meanings and symbols attached to your glands, brain, bones, blood, and all the rest of you. This is the path into the kingdoms attached to the different parts of you, where you can play or heal or learn.
To observe the truth about one's self relies on introspection. This means developing the ability to recapitulate (taking a self inventory) and accept one's life so far; to accept and become objective about it. The Earth element helps us develop true depth of meaning in this manner.

ω When working with the earth element, one becomes more reliable, dependable, and responsible; more balanced in every part of their life.

ω One becomes able to keep their word.

ω One becomes more self-reliant, emotionally, physically, mentally, and in every way.

ω Ones bodies become more aware of each other and begin to work together.

ω One becomes more objective about the world around them.

The following desirable character traits may be developed by working with the Earth element:

¬ patience
¬ tolerance
¬ neatness
¬ sobriety
¬ inner taste and smell
¬ punctuality
¬ The ability to discern the truth.
¬ A deep respect for the beauty of growth and expansion of awareness
¬ a reverence for the physical aspects of life
¬ The ability to heal in the physical.

Placements and symbols of the Earth Element:

The earth element governs from the mid thigh down in the physical body.

¬ The season of year symbolizing the Earth Element is the winter season.

¬ Its direction is north
¬ Temperature is cold
¬ Its food is meat and proteins
¬ The time of day is deep night until dawn
¬ It is the time of the teaching of wisdom
¬ Percussion instruments, echoes, yodels
¬ The home of the Element of wisdom
¬ The third finger on the left hand is the earth finger-ring finger
¬ Gnomes, goblins, trolls, elves, earth creatures, more
¬ Earth colors- browns, blacks, yellows

Positive Earth Element:

It is through the earth element that one's desires and goals are manifested.

¬ The learning of objectivity about one's self
¬ Development of inner courage
¬ Consideration for others
¬ Resoluteness
¬ loving firmness
¬ neatness
¬ cleanness
¬ self confidence
¬ self assuredness
¬ sobriety

Negative Earth element:

When the Earth element manifests negatively, one can't get anything done.

¬ The inability to complete projects
¬ Irresponsibility
¬ Rebellion
¬ antagonism towards authority and the laws that govern life

- ¬ atheist attitudes
- ¬ lack of belief in a higher power
- ¬ defiance
- ¬ belligerent behavior
- ¬ dullness
- ¬ laziness
- ¬ unclean about self and environment
- ¬ an unscrupulous and calculating mind

The Earth element holds the keys to the answers to the problems which arise while humans exist on the astral plane.

Not enough Earth Elements:

Running out of trace minerals indicates a lack of earth element in the physical body.

- ¬ In the chest area- heart murmurs
- ¬ loss of hair in the male
- ¬ Brittle bones
- ¬ ungrounded behavior
- ¬ fatigue
- ¬ lack of interest in sex
- ¬ no sex drive
- ¬ sexual impotency

Too much Earth element:

Can cause one to feel like they have a heavy head, like they are walking through molasses
to become preoccupied with outer forms
to become constipated
 inability to eliminate waste in the physical
carrying of grudges
emotional blocks
heavy fatigue on any level

absent mindedness
lust
isolation

The Water Element

The Arch (Arc) Angel who administers the energies of the Water Element is Gabriel.

The Archangel Gabriel administers the energies of the water element. She/He governs all of the astral planes of energy in human divinity. Gabriel is the "Divine Messenger of God.
"Gabriel" means "Strong one of God."
She/He was the Archangel of both the Annunciation and the Resurrection.
It is She/He who is the conscious carrier between the Divine and human intelligence. The strongest connection to this kind of consciousness resides in the higher mental planes, the higher causal body, and the lower soul planes.

Gabriel is closely associated with the Lunar tides and the Waters of life.
Gabriel is the Life Bearer; powered by the strength of life.
As the cup is the symbol of Gabriel, so we ourselves are cups containing consciousness and life, with our hearts receiving the Divine Spark. Love, with its double polarity, like the cup, both holds and pours out, and comforts and cheers.
Gabriel governs rebirth through the Sacrament of Baptism and personifies the creative powers of life.
IIc is the Communion bearer, and the Key Holder of the Floodgates of the place we call Heaven.
Gabriel works with the water element to link the energies which connect all life forms.
Gabriel is the Ruler of Purification.
When we begin to draw the spiritual energies down through the energy levels that make up our bodies, with the purpose of bringing those energies into our consciousness, we have to have cleaned up the vessels, the bodies those higher spiritual vibrations will pour down through and into.
To draw the spiritual energies that carry a higher vibration down

through one's bodies, one must remove the energy blocks that lie in the way. One will hurt themselves and get blasted by those energies, if they don't do the work to clean out the energy blocks in the bodies, cleaning out; thus raising their vibrations so that they can gradually draw the spiritual energies safely down through their bodies without harm. That takes deliberately doing your emotional work and clearing and cleaning it up.

Character development is spiritual development. It is to be done through a harmonious blending of both the energies that are moving down through one, and the energies moving upward through one.

The Water Element:

The water element is associated with the astral, the emotional body.
> The season symbolizing the water element is spring
> Its direction is east.
> Temperature is warm
> Colors- silver, sky blue
> Sense- feeling
> The time of day is early morning.
> It is the time of the learning and teaching of the child, both inner and outer. That means both polarities. The learning of the ability to keep the astral body in balance.
> Stimulation of mans' intelligence and intuition.

The Water Element makes children curious, both inner and outer, therefore can transform the energy of Empowering Love into manifest form.

- ¬ The water element is the most feminine of the four lower elements, having a four-sided negative or magnetic polarity. Polarity is 4 x negative.
- ¬ This element is responsible for working with human kind's nervous system

¬ Healing emotional difficulties requires the water element
¬ Foods are:
  o waters
  o liquids
  o creams
  o sauces
  o sea foods
¬ Sounds:
  o bells
  o cymbals
  o chimes
¬ Symbols:
  o cup
  o cauldron
  o chalice.
¬ Senses:
  o Hearing

Smell- Smell is the Merman, the Father of Travel

Water Elementals are Mermaids, Undines, water creatures
¬ Little finger
¬ The water element governs all birthings and all beginnings of any kind
¬ The Water element governs reproduction of life, regeneration and sexuality. These energies are all dependent upon the fluid motions that go on throughout all the bodies.
¬ The water element assists in the uses of the mind and utilizing The Higher Intellect, can heal cuts and wounds and injuries, and all mental disorders.
¬ The water element is attuned to the feminine aspects of Nature.

Some of the positive abilities you will develop when working with the Water element are:

Positive gains to your character development

- ¬ Inventiveness, the linking of questions to their answers
- ¬ The ability to feel on the inner
- ¬ Modesty
- ¬ the ability to forgive
- ¬ comprehension
- ¬ Serenity
- ¬ Compassion
- ¬ Devotion
- ¬ Tenderness
- ¬ Respectability
- ¬ Seriousness
- ¬ a zest for life
- ¬ the ability to meditate
- ¬ the ability to act quickly
- ¬ comprehension- increased perception
- ¬ The remembrance of dreams.
- ¬ Cleansing and purifying on all levels
- ¬ Stimulation of the intellect through questioning motives and intention
- ¬ revealing the future for yourself and others
- ¬ revelation of the essence of lessons to be learned
- ¬ development of intuition
- ¬ Magnetic appeal and charisma
- ¬ laughter
- ¬ joy
- ¬ development of imagination
- ¬ development of psychic abilities
- ¬ increased perception of others' reasons for doing things
- ¬ stimulation of the desire to grow
- ¬ release of creativity
- ¬ the ability to feel our desires

The development of curiosity: **Curiosity** speeds up lower-case sight- bridge of nose- lower keys of hearing-Sinus- neuralgia.

One can come to learn the sacred meaning of water and symbiosis, for water carries the emotions.
When working with the water element, you will learn about the power of purification rituals, and about the structure of all rituals.

When the Water Element becomes negatively polarized it can manifest in:
- Brooding
- Laziness
- Shyness
- indifference or being passive
- all forms of depression
- being a loner, withdrawn, as in all forms of introversions and all their manifestations
- lethargy, lack of emotional motion, "I don't care" because I don't have enough energy to care.

Too much water element can cause:

- Constant emotional over-reactions
- a tendency to always be sad or tearful
- despondent
- depressed
- an inability to release, to let go, being obsessive
- In the physical body, too much water element can cause water retention and bloating
- bladder and kidney problems
- high cholesterol

Not enough water element may cause:

- The inability to feel emotions or to emotionally relate to anyone or anything for varying periods of time.
- An inaccurate sense of not being connected to life
- Gullible, a lack of perception

A person who lacks these energies could be mistakenly referred to as frivolous, empty headed, fake, narrow minded, mindless, silly, short sighted.

Physically, not enough water element can show up as chapped lips, dry skin, thirst, wrinkles, a temper. The simple remedy is to drink more water and be around it more.

The Water element carries a magnetic charge and is the mediating agent between fire and air because both the fire and air elements carry a positive polarity.

The Air Element

The Arch Angel who administers the Air Element is Ralphael.

Ralphael represents the basic forces of the Sun.
It is through the Archangel Ralphael and his/her teachings that we develop a conscience and begin to understand and sense the differences between right and wrong.

Ralphael is the Great Teacher and the Healer of mankind. His/her name means "Healing of God".
He/She teaches us how to make use of our minds, and to understand that the mind is an instrument and a means of serving God. In the physical, this connection operates through our brain.

Ralphael is known for his Wit and Wisdom, and it is this he tries to pass on to humanity.
It is through Ralphael's endeavors that our knowledge and love of God is strengthened, and with this comes the dawning of our inner light and life.

The Caduceus is his symbol of healing.

His greatest power is in the healing of wounds and of mental illnesses.

His arrows are the protection of travelers.

His double-edged sword severs the silver chord when it is time; the life giving linkage from the higher self down to the physical body. One side of his sword symbolizes the outer, human consciousness, the other side symbolizes the inner divine consciousness.
The tip of the sword combines and blends the two, just as Ralphael attempts to help humankind to unite their inner and

outer life into a whole through knowledge and healing.

The ability to express the truth, to express any truth, depends on the air element, and how much or little of it, and what kind you have of it, and in what body.

The air element aids in breathing with the purpose of bringing spiritual energies into the other bodies, as well as aiding the physical body. If you practice breathing too hard, too deep or too much on purpose, you might prematurely open chakras or energy centers that are not ready yet.

The Air Element is associated with the mental body.

The Air Element:

- Its season is fall
- Its direction is west
- Temperature is cool
- Food are bread and honeycomb
- Time of day is dusk
- It is the teaching of structuring
- restructuring, and organizing
- It is associated with the mental body
- Symbols for the air element are
    - bells
    - swords
    - woodwind instruments
    - brass horns
- It is associated with the Sense of hearing.
- Elementals- Works with fairies and Sylphs
- The Fairy Bible

When working with the positive air element, one can further the development of the following positive abilities:

- ¬ The ability to focus, to concentrate
- ¬ diligence
- ¬ Strengthens the understanding of the connection between the inner and the outer
- ¬ Allows one to become introspective and learn the dignity of sadness
- ¬ Allows one to give up their long-standing grief
- ¬ develops cheerfulness
- ¬ Joyfulness
- ¬ kindness
- ¬ optimism
- ¬ thought independence
- ¬ cleverness
- ¬ competence
- ¬ advances the development of inner hearing and smell
- ¬ advances the ability to understand complexities, result is a keener and quicker mind

Some of the negative aspects of the air element are:

- ¬ depression
- ¬ can't finish a thought
- ¬ can't concentrate on anything
- ¬ lack of stamina, hardiness, durability
- ¬ scorn, disgust, repugnance for others
- ¬ unreasonably distrustful, suspicious without a cause
- ¬ lacking in integrity, cheating, dishonesty
- ¬ don't have what it takes to maintain a lasting relationship
- ¬ talks constantly
- ¬ A dull mind, can't think, too much effort, slow thinking

Too much air element can cause:

- ¬ uncontrollable, obsessive, fanatical behaviors

- ¬ dry skin
- ¬ Constant hunger in the physical body, indicating that there is not enough of solar prauna (food) coming in. Need to draw in more air element for this
- ¬ excessive mental activity
- ¬ lack of sleep, over stimulated from too much air element
- ¬ a desire to deceive, control and influence others
- ¬ taking over conversations
- ¬ justifying everything to a fault

Not enough air element can cause:

- ¬ Telling lies
- ¬ Can't express ideas to others
- ¬ Slow, dulled thinking, and scattering of thoughts
- ¬ Lying to one's self to avoid responsibility
- ¬ Projection, someone else did it, you didn't, it's not you
- ¬ adjusting your principles in order to compromise
- ¬ A feeling as though you can't hear the sounds you need to
- ¬ People sound like they are talking from far away
- ¬ Can't finish what you start.

When one doesn't have enough air element, if it becomes chronic, people might perceive them as not mentally stable, whether they are or not.

The Fire Element

The Arch Angel who administers the Fire element is Michael, Lord of the Angels.

Ralphael and Michael both are assigned to the Sun.

Michael is the Leader of the Heavenly Hosts, the Prince of Light. His name means "Perfect of God."

- He is the Carrier of the Fire
- He is the Bearer of Light and Illumination
- Michael is closely associated with Protection, Perfection, and Power
- His Sword is pointed downward in Peace, joining the Earth in this Purpose
- Michael is in charge of all of the Angelic activities
- Michael personifies Right and Reason, triumphing over Wrong and Ignorance
- Michael feels that Evil is a condition of unbalance, and with his help, good is produced through Harmony and Balance

This Harmony is the cohesive power of Michael, which holds the Universe in perfect balance.

As Ralphael is the Healer of Wounds and Injuries, Michael is The Healer of Disease, which are many times, caused by Dis-harmony.

- Michael is the Great Intercessor for all of humanity
- Michael works with intelligence and reason, power and light, and understanding on a soul level
- He/She is the Healer of organic diseases that manifest as a result of dis-harmony

- ¬ Michael represents the solar forces aspects of spiritual power. He represents the solar Hero who guards the approaches to Consciousness from Negative Fire.

Michael contains all the electric fluids, and represents the Masculine Principle throughout all of Nature.

He imparts both the sacred and mundane heats and warmth to the physical body.

Heat is made possible through this element.

The polarity of the fire element is positive-positive. The fire element is the most positive, the most masculine of the four lower elements.

- ¬ Symbolizing the fire element:
- ¬ Temperature is hot
- ¬ Earth placements:
  - o deserts
  - o tropics
  - o volcanos'
- ¬ Sense of sight
- ¬ Spicy foods, peppers, hot foods
- ¬ Colors are red orange. The fire element moves with force, as does the color energy red.
- ¬ The Index finger is the fire finger. Mothers point this finger at their children.
- ¬ Season - summer
- ¬ Time of day- noon- it is the time of the teaching of knowledge
- ¬ Direction- south (where the heat is)
- ¬ Sounds:
  - o the rod,
  - o harp
  - o all String instruments
- ¬ Salamanders

¬ This Element is associated with the soul body.
¬ It is with the Fire element that we do our major expression, that being from the soul planes and above.
¬ It is through the fire element that dynamic motivations manifest, and through them, the positive forces of magic align.

Some of the positive aspects of the fire element:

The Fire element is the most important of all of the energies for the expansion of the soul. It is through the Fire element that our soul wakes up and begins to produce certain energies and grow.

¬ When working with the fire element in its positive aspects, we begin to manifest an enthusiasm and a zest for life.
¬ We learn how to protect ourselves and others.
¬ We begin to be aware of what's going on in the inner planes of ourselves and others.
¬ We become better people as we expand into more awareness of our higher self and others higher selves.
¬ We are able to affect more of Life.
¬ We are able to do more.
¬ We develop a vigorous, forceful, powerful understanding and courage.

The Fire Element can help one travel through the lower planes of energy, and enter the higher planes of energy. This requires the development of the will.

Remember to release all excess fire energy often when working with it, so that the masculine nature is not over stimulated. It easily becomes over stimulated.

The fire element transmutes, changes, converts, alters the energy. It always transforms the energy. That is its job.

So you can't go back, only forwards. The fire element is a point of transformation energy. It is a shield and can be used with other things, and usually is.

When the fire element becomes negatively polarized, some of the manifestations are:

- Pessimism
- Sarcasm
- Caustic humor
- Irritability
- Fiery or short temper
- jealousy
- destructive tendencies
- extreme self-destructive behavior- Release the excess fire element regularly to interrupt this pattern.

Not enough fire element may manifest as:

- Not enough stimulation-manifests in a lack of motivation
- Indifferent, spiritless
- Inability to commit emotionally to anything
- Lethargy in the physical
- Sleeping too much
- Passive aggressive behaviors
- Extreme procrastination
- Extreme stubbornness

Too much Fire element may manifest as:

- Over active, too stimulated
- inability to concentrate because of excess scattering of energies
- storing of tension in the neck and head
- obnoxious behaviors, headaches, fevers

¬ nervousness, all kinds of irritations
¬ irritation of the physical body, like rashes, itches, hives,
  etc.

Each of these elemental manifestations occur in one of the four energy bodies and on different sub planes, so choose the element that works with that body when you look at that manifestation.

The Fifth Element and Its Chakras:

The Four Lower Elements work with the Color energies to maintain the seven chakras and meridian energy systems located throughout our physical, astral, mental and soul bodies. But there are at least five chakras outside of our bodies that revolve around our head; that are energetically attached to the upper occipital ridge, cranial plates, and crown chakras of our heads. They are located outside our bodies because their energy is too fast to stay in the lower realms of the Matter we are made of.

The Fifth Element, the Ether Element:

Aristotle described the fifth element, Ether, as the unseen element. Aristotle described it as filling all the space that wasn't filled by the four lower elements.

The Ether Element is the Eternal Mass

- Aither is a primordial Deity. He is one of the first born Elementals and embodies the pure Upper Air that God breathes. Pronounced Aether or Aither in Greek, Akmon in Latin, or Akashic Element in India, and Ether in Western Philosophies.
- Thoreal is the Archangel of the Ether Element.
- The Ether element is a cloudy white color, and works with our middle finger, the longest finger on our hand.
- The Ether Element is the space between molecules that gives them the opportunity to create Form. It is the God energy.

The Ether Element carries the vitality of Spirit (not religion) into all parts of our being and infuses all parts of life with it. In this place, we are all one. It is the place where we experience what relationship really means. That happens through the Ether Element.

It is through the Ether Element that all planes of existence are interconnected. If you have enough Ether Element, you see more than the details of Life, you begin to comprehend the context in which life is lived.

Every atom in our bodies is connected by space. There is an atom and space, another atom, and space around it. That space between atoms is the Ether element.

Chemists know that the Ether element is to be found in all forms of life. They don't know exactly how it works, but they know it is there. It is everywhere, and for that reason, it is called the God Element.
The specific region of the physical body for the ether element is the center of the spine, and of lesser concentration, the entire body.

As energy becomes faster, it loses matter and rises. The atoms are farther apart, which causes the colors to lose their density and become paler. Coming down through the energy planes, the color energies get darker as they pick up matter.

The Higher Chakras

Along with the seven major chakras most metaphysical teachings tell us we have, we also have chakras outside of our bodies that are connected to us. We have at least five chakras (and no doubt, more,) that are energetically aligned with the ridges in the upper occipital lobe of the head, and they are attached at strategic areas to the Etheric body and to the causal bodies of all manifested Matter on this planet. That includes human beings.

We live and die just as the stars in the cosmos do. To track the birth and magnificent death of a star is to track our own beginning and endings. We are birthed and live and begin to fade just as stars do. We are a part of the larger law of All. Everything

47

we know about is a part of the larger law of All. And so, we must
be fed vital cosmic energies:

- ¬ Universal
- ¬ Galactic
- ¬ Galactic Super cluster
- ¬ Solar system
- ¬ Sun
- ¬ Planetary

This happens through the chakra system. The cosmic collection
of energies is fed to our Etheric web through the outer chakras
that gravitate outside of, and around our head and bodies.

The cosmic chakras constantly remind our individual life force
what the universe means to us; they remind us that we are a part
of the universe and are connected to it at all times.

The five chakras define our place in the larger scheme of Life.

They feed consistent, measured doses of the Greater Nature of
Life to us so that we can maintain the deeper understanding of
the Greater Forces we are a part of. The five outer chakras
connect us to our Cosmic Elders.

The Etheric body and the cosmic chakras

The Etheric body works with the Ether Element. It looks like a
net or web surrounding ourselves. No one knows exactly how far
out it is from our bodies, but we can estimate that it is fluid,
flexible, and within a few inches of our physical body.

Each of the cosmic energy chakras works with a different part of
the Etheric body, the energy body, the web or net that surrounds
us. When the Etheric body is rent or torn or damaged in some
way, it takes spiritual energy to get to it and do the work to heal
it because its vibration is so high. The Etheric body resides
where it does, it has very little matter, and is fluidic and delicate
because of it.

Spiritual rituals or spiritual ceremonies are needed to pave the way to Etheric body healing. This is because the energy has to be high enough in vibration to reach the Etheric healing area, and spiritual applications raise energy.

Think of the Etheric web or a grid, with cross points. Seated at each cross point is a spinning sphere containing and maintaining a small amount of chemical mix of colors and elements, just suited for you, that came from the stars in the universe a long time ago.

The third eye and the cosmic chakras

Under the third eye sits a hologram of the Earth. It is located at the bridge of the nose in human beings. This hologram seats the third eye into Earth's dimensions and grounds it there. It is your identity map that allows the cosmic chakras to attach to and work in Earth dimensions. This hologram also identifies you as to where you are located in this universe and on this earth.

The cosmic chakras are connected to the upper occipital ridge and from there, their energies are transported faster than the speed of light, (which includes other time dimensions), into portals running from your cranial plates and out to about 18 inches around your face, like a mask of energy.

Your sense of smell and sight is faster than any of your other senses. These are the senses that regulate the speed of, and send these energies into the rest of the system.

We stay connected to the cosmos through the intervention of these outer chakras. The Universe is 13.8 billion years old. The Earth is 4 and a half billion years old.

These chakras spin faster than the seven physical body chakras. That is why they reside outside of the physical body. They have to reside outside of the body because of their higher vibration. They spin faster, in order to maintain the linkage between us and the universal energies. These chakras embody and maintain for each of us, the Law that All Life lives by, so that All can continue to exist.

The five chakras are faster moving than our physical, mental, astral, and soul bodies. That means that we have a permanent connection to the cosmos that lasts after we transcend our physical bodies.

To study the cosmos is to learn how our higher beginnings and endings take place.

We are truly Star material…

We are birthed just as the stars are, and so we must go through an aging and death process. We do this to refine and collect the best of ourselves for our next adventure in the cosmos, just as the stars do.

To become spiritually independent, one must work with the elements.

- ¬ When working with the elemental energies one becomes more self reliant in each body. Better relationships are established between the bodies.
- ¬ One becomes more able to take on more personal responsibility.
- ¬ One becomes more able to see what is going on from an objective point of view.
- ¬ Elements help a person to get in touch with the truth about themselves.
- ¬ Elements help one become more balanced in every part of their life.

It is through the elemental energies that the higher abilities of humankind are able to manifest in a balanced manner.
You will learn that you are responsible for containing your own energy around others.

That hearing is utilized to monitor connection, equilibrium, direction, and centering. Imagine, visualize, analyze.

The electron unites, connects, and makes construction possible.

It is the mother principle at work. It is the power of silence.

The elements work differently on every energy plane with the principles of connection and receiving.

The patterning for, and the way we have been trained to use the force of fusion, is given to us by our mother, through our relationship with her.

The energies of the elements can be used to release, allowing us to experience and express from a positive polarity. We can be sad, angry, happy, etc. from a positive polarity.

Elemental properties and a few of their associations:

1. Unconditional Love and freedom-Das Kaishn a Master of Heaven and Spirit- Uranus- The Fool
2. Illusion and reality:
     o   Hermes
     o   Mercury
     o   The magician
3. Creative Wisdom:
     o   Isis
     o   Moon
     o   the High Priestess
4. Abundance:
     o   Aphrodite
     o   Venus
     o   the Empress
5. Power and authority
     o   Osiris-Hercules
     o   Jehovah

- o   Aries
- o   the Emperor
6. Spiritual Understanding:
- o   the Grand Master
- o   Taurus
7. Loving relationships
- o   Anubis
- o   Gemini
- o   the Lovers
8. Victory and triumph
- o   Serapis
- o   Cancer
- o   the Chariot
9. Order and harmony
- o   Athena
- o   Minerva
- o   Libra
- o   Justice
10. Discernment
- o   Adonis
- o   Virgo
- o   the Hermit
11. Cycles and solutions-
- o   Zeus
- o   Jupiter
- o   Wheel of Fortune
12. Spiritual strength and will
- o   daughter of Leo-
- o   Strength-
- o   the Flaming Sword
13. Renunciation and regeneration-
- o   Poseidon-
- o   Neptune-
- o   the hanged man
14. Death and rebirth
- o   Tharnatos
- o   death

    o   Scorpio
15. Patience and acceptance
    o   Iris
    o   queen of heaven
16. Sagittarius-temperance-
    o   hips
    o   thighs
    o   liver
17. Materiality-and temptation
    o   Janus the tempter
    o   Capricorn
    o   Pan
18. Knees, bones, joints, rheumatism, arthritis

Etheric Web Healing Ritual

Here is simple way to work on the Etheric web. Do this for just a few minutes. Do not linger or ask questions.

Raise your vibrations ahead of time before doing this by cleaning your physical body, bathing, no deodorants or perfumes or makeup. Be as natural as you can; wear cotton or other natural fibers. Don't do this right after eating. Try to fast for a few hours first.

Stand and take a spiritual stance of some kind. If you can't do it physically, imagine yourself doing it. You can get someone to take a stance for you, too.

Imagine you are diving deep down into the Earth. Go down, down, down, until you are diving through earthy red clay. As you dive, feel the Earth stripping the negative away from you.

Then turn and fly straight back up to the Earth's surface and stand on it. Spread your arms out in thanksgiving for the cleanliness you now have. Your feet are like roots in the Earth, and you and the Earth are both glad. (Now you are in alignment with each other) This won't last long.

Look down in front of you. You have brought back a container of beautiful, dark red Earth mud with you. Close your eyes and go to your etheric web and find any rents and tears. Surprise! You brought the mud back with you. Begin using the luscious, easily molded mud to repair any rents or tears. Very soon, this window of opportunity will close. It lasts a short time. The word luscious is used on purpose, as it is a word indicating a lovely fat content, and this mud has Earth oils in it.

Look your progress over. You may not be finished, so you will have to come back another time and work on the rest of it. Wait at least three days before you do this ritual again, for the Earth Elements do not get in alignment with you at your beck and call. Check your etheric web for any problems and get familiar with where they are located, so that when the elements (Cosmic and Earth) allow you to work there, you won't have to spend time locating the areas to be healed. You can go right to them and set to work. Always thank the Earth and Cosmic forces when you end the ritual. And state, "Let this healing be done in the highest good of all."

The Electron in Atomic Structure; The Practicioners of Feminine Spirituality

On this planet, The Mystery Schools as well as many Indigenous peoples and Pagans work with the development of the inner Elemental kingdoms.

The Elemental beings work with the Great Mysteries residing within the electron cloud residing within the inner world of each atom of our being.

Pythagoras, Plato, and Plotinus were members of Mystery Schools.

Most Mystery Schools affirm ancient origins. Eight thousand years ago the Goddess Cybele was worshipped as the Magna Mater in a Mystery School.

The Mystery Religions were outlawed by the patriarchal religions because their schools of thought concerning hierarchies of power and their maintenance, were distinctly different.

The Spiritual Practitioners of the Circle: Pagans

The white circles in magic practices are there to separate one's energies from another's. For your protection and theirs.

Paganism is the oldest Spiritual practice known to humanity. Its origins are undocumented, but it is believed to be the last remnants of the Spiritual beliefs of the last Matriarchal Era. Paganism has no founder or founders, no earthly leaders, nor beliefs that rely on human beings, no prophets, no messiahs, no saints.
The word "Pagan" is derived from the Latin word Paganus, meaning a civilian, and from Pagus, meaning a village. While the

majority of Pagans live in a town these days, this term accurately describes the Pagan heritage and the affinity they feel with the natural environment.

The First Pagan Oath

I will be ever more true to the will of the Goddess, to the Codes of the Warriors, and the lives of the People.
I will be Mighty against the Mighty
Gentle to the Weak
Generous to the Poor
Merciless to the Rapacious
I will do nothing of which I may be ashamed, but seek no Honor.
I will give no less Justice to others and seek no more for myself
I will be Valiant in Adversity and humble in Prosperity
I will live with Joy and I will die Bravely wherever I am.

Pagans and the other indigenous groups on this planet revered and followed the concepts that were vital to sustaining life in bygone times.
Pagans have kept these principles and adapted their use to modern times.
Pagans are people who follow a path of individual Spiritual growth that is in harmony with the Earth upon which we live. Pagans are from all cultures, all ages, and all races. Pagans study the past. All ancestors are revered.

Pagans have an inborn respect for this planet and are aware of their connection to it. Many of their Spiritual Paths emphasize the equality of men and women, though some Pagan traditions are specifically geared towards exploring the male or female Mysteries.
These ways of being are also true for Native Americans, the Inuits, many African peoples, and others in South America and around the world.
This way of thinking is not a religion. Paganism is not a religion. Religions are highly structured groups that depend on a Mediator

and a sky god. Christianity, Catholicism, the Jewish faith, Islam, all the world religions, employ strict sets of rules that eliminate and diminish the importance of the feminine nature of life.

Pagan traditions break down into various groups with different beliefs and practices, depending on the origin and culture. All of them work with the cycles of the Moon instead of the Sun. Pagan time frames move counter-clockwise, and all their calendars are based on the Moon cycles.

Here are some types of Pagan practices:

- Asa Tru/ Norse Paganism
  Originated in northern Europe, feels an affinity towards Nordic and Teutonic ancestors, studies the Sagas, Eddas, and Runes. This is a context of Noble Warrior Traditions, encouraging responsibility and growth.

- Celtic Paganism
  Native to Celtic and Gaelic races and where those originated. Ireland, Wales, England, that area. This is an oral tradition. The essence and teachings of the ancient traditions were encoded into songs and ballads and stories and transmitted orally to the people.

- Dianic Witchcraft
  A tradition which honors and celebrates the feminine aspect of Divinity. Women are accorded great respect and rituals are often designed to empower women with a sense of their own inherent spirituality and values.

- Druidic/ Druidry
  The emphasis is on music and poetry. This practice is a branch of the Celtic and Gaelic traditions. They are academic, and their symbol is the tree. Druids believe that souls are immortal, and that after a definite number of years, they live a second life after the soul passes into another body.

Julius Caesar said of the Druids, " The cardinal doctrine which they seek to teach is that souls do not die, but after death, pass from one to another, and this belief, as the fear of death is thereby cast aside, they hold to be the greatest invective to Valor. "

ϖ Solitary Pagans
Solitary Pagans actively work to save the Earth from desecration. They honor the land we live on as the sacred living mother of humanity. There are no formal rites or methods of worship. Pagans encourage each individual to honor divinity by caring for the Earth and all its creatures.

Hellenic, Roman, and Egyptian
Hellenic, Roman, and Egyptian Paganism is the practice of particular ethics within groups. Some of these practices are Voodoo, Santa Ria, Native American Traditions, and Aborigines. Many of the traditions of indigenous peoples in this group have been lost through contact with uncompromising religious missionaries and settlers.

ϖ Shamanism
Birth, death, and healing, and connection of the circle through ancestors. Shamanic practices are also used today in non-tribal societies.

ϖ Wicca
Wicca perceives Divinity in the form of the Goddess and God, each one having many different aspects. They hold meetings in accordance with the Moon and have eight festivals a year celebrating the different aspects of the Goddess and God. Wiccans believe in "Summerland" a place where souls play and learn and rest before being reborn into the physical world.

ϖ Witchcraft

Is the popular revival of European witchcraft, an ancient fertility religion. Honors the horned God and Goddess. Called the Old Religion, practitioners use herbs and are healers. Their practices and techniques are similar to tribal Shamanism and the village Wise Woman.

Pagans believe that the Diety are everywhere and imminent, both here and now, and transcendent.

¬ Deity is a part of the fabric of our being, of our environment, and of that which is beyond anything we can imagine. Deity is perceived as both male and female.

¬ All things are in their own place therefore, they should be in harmony. No extremism.

¬ Pagans believe in re-incarnation. There is a strong belief in cyclical life patterns, which do not cease, with or without the death of the physical body.

¬ Pagans have no concept that could be described as heaven or Hell as Christians do.

The Norse or Northern Pagan traditions do have their own complex, sophisticated version of heaven and hell that involves resting places where different kinds of transformations take place on the journey. The final resting place is alive and wise, and full of new adventures for them to have.

Each Pagan tradition has its own philosophy about the afterlife and about reincarnation. Pagans have individual beliefs and philosophies about these subjects, as Paganism does not have a dogma, or strict set of teachings which all pagans must follow, like religions do.

¬ Paganism is one of the "Mystery" Paths, in which each individual has direct experience - one on one, of Divinity.

¬ Paganism is becoming a more common practice. Although it is becoming more common for pagan priests and priestesses to perform rites for a group of people, individual experience of Divinity remains the primary objective for pagans.

¬ Pagan practice differs significantly from most state religions where a figure or an authority head performs the rites and mediates the divine force on behalf of a congregation. In most pagan practices, each individual is a priest or priestess in their own right.

¬ Pagans do not worship trees or rocks: They revere the divine force contained within them, and in each part of the universe.

¬ Pagans do not worship a savior or other spiritual leaders. The emphasis is on each individual's spiritual enlightenment. The practice of paganism is a voyage of self discovery to find one's own place within the divine realms.

¬ Pagans believe that each individual has the right to and should worship in their own way. There is no required legislation for a prescribed manner of worship. Some prefer to worship privately, others in groups.

¬ Pagan rites of passage
  o birth
  o marriage
  o death
  o initiations
  o events are designed to create spiritual awakenings.

- Pagan practices do not include animal or human sacrifice, nor any activity which is against the wishes or ethics of the initiated.
- Birth rituals include a naming ceremony, but do not promise the named to a religion.
  - Birth rituals- the practice is to ask for divine guidance and protection for the named by someone acting as parents. There are no promises made to bring the child up in a particular faith. The child is free to choose.
- It is a strong Pagan belief that each individual must follow his or her own path.
- Children are taught to honor their family and friends and to have integrity and honesty. To treat the Earth as sacred. To love and respect all forms of life. Questioning and quests are encouraged to develop their own spirituality.
- Children are exposed on purpose to a number of religious teachings that gives a well balanced spiritual education, feeding the soul therefore, and allowing more personal choice.
- There are no dietary requirements - those who follow a vegetarian dict or abstain from alcohol, tobacco, etc., do so out of choice, not as a tenet of faith.
- There are no laws of blasphemy. Conflict between individuals remains the responsibility of those who are involved.
- Paganism does not legislate where matters of loyalty and ethics are concerned. There is no penance, nor other forms of religious punishment.
- Each individual is taught to be responsible for their sexual activity, procreation, use of alcohol and other mind-altering substances.
- Pagans have a high regard for the equality of the sexes. They do not suppress the feminine principle in the way that other practices do. Pagan priestesses have the same status as Pagan priests.

¬ Acknowledged, accepted concept of Elders defined as those from the community who, by virtue of training and experience, have a greater understanding of social, moral, and practical matters.

    o These elders prescribe behaviors.

¬ Children are sacred to Pagans. Paganism is a legitimate, coherent, and responsible spiritual path to which many people are attracted in these days of ecological concerns.

¬ Pagans believe that every day is holy. There are many festivals throughout the Pagan system. The festivals are based on the moon, the turning of the seasons, and the solstices and equinoxes.

The year is divided into two halves, dark and light. Marriage was forbidden during the dark half. Samhain or Halloween, began the dark half of the year, with Beltane, or May Day beginning the light half of the year.

¬ There are two Solstice and two Equinox celebrations.

    o The Winter Solstice-Dec. 21 or 22 or 23, is the day of the year that has the most dark in it. The longest night and the shortest day.

    o The Summer Solstice-June 20-22, is the day of the year that has the most light in it. It is the longest day and the shortest night of the year.

    o The two Equinoxes have equal amounts of light and day in them.

    o The Vernal Equinox- Day and night stand equal

    o The Autumnal Equinox- Night and day stand equal

The Pagan calendar runs counter clockwise around the Circle. The New Year begins on October 31, through November 1 and 2, Samhain or Halloween.

The New Year starts at sunset on Oct. 31. and continues through Nov. 2nd.

This gave the people time to recapitulate the past year, to settle old grievances, and to go into the next year with a new outlook. Thinning of the veils start at the dark of the moon before and goes through the 2nd, before the veil shuts again. This is a lunar festival.

Lunar Festival
- o Considered the Festival of the Dead.
- o Ombole
- o Feb. 1,2,3. -One of the four fire, or Solar Festivals. The rekindled sun was welcomed, bringing the earliest hopes of spring. The winter of old age starts to give way to youth and birth. Honors the Goddess Brigid. Brigantia- Ombole- time of birthing of lambs and ewes-time of milk- female festival.
- o Candlemas- candles in caldron to burn away the night and let in the sun- first melt of the snow- celebrated with milk and wheat-awareness that spring is coming

Beltane
- o May 1,2,3-last spring festival - fertility festival -a time when the veil is thinnest again- a veil time usually ignored and unknown by most
  Weisak Festival - lunar festival - May day - time of purification - the yearly fertility Festival welcoming summer. Marks the beginning of the light half of the year.

Lammas- Lughnassagh
- o Aug 1 and 2 - start of harvest- marks end of fighting season - warriors' festival - put down all weapons and harvest the grain - male festival - weapons contests - celebrate God - shining one, god of light - festival for guardians, it is the only time they can let their hair down.

Lugnassadh – female -harvest festival celebrating the wedding of Lugh to Mother Earth. A proper time for marriage. A funerary rite as the sun starts his long journey into winter.

The divisions of Elemental Matter are called Kingdoms. In each Kingdom, there are Elemental Hierarchies.

The four Directions:
- ϖ **North.** Purposeful building of shields,
  - white
  - mind
  - logic
  - wisdom
  - animals
  - harmony
  - balance
  - air
  - earth element - gray, brown green or black, dwarfs, gnomes, trolls
- ϖ **South.** fire element
  - Yellow, red Orange
  - salamanders
  - dragons
  - red
  - trust
  - innocence
  - little boys and girls
  - plant
  - emotion
  - fear
  - anger
  - love
- ϖ **West.** Water element
  - Blue gray and sometimes sea green,
  - undines

- o Mer people
- o black
- o minerals
- o mother Earth
- o death
- o change
- o introspection
- o where we hold our adult spirit shields
- ϖ **East.** Air element
  - o Yellow
  - o white
  - o sylphs
  - o fairies
  - o gold or yellow
  - o humans
  - o soul fire
  - o child spirit shield

Elemental Kingdoms:
- ϖ N. governs
  - o weather
  - o place of wealth
  - o snow
  - o death
  - o wisdom
  - o earth power
  - o infancy
- ϖ E. governs
  - o knowledge
  - o illumination
  - o love
  - o wisdom
  - o spirituality/ spirit world
  - o air power
  - o old age

- ϖ W.governs
  - o life
  - o wisdom
  - o middle age
  - o healing
  - o maturity
  - o water power
- ϖ S. governs
  - o war
  - o vengeance
  - o healing
  - o rage
  - o lust
  - o wisdom
  - o youth
  - o fire power

"Widdershins" is the Celtic and Wiccan word for clockwise. "Widdershins" rituals are for invoking, building of energy, life. "Deosil" is the word for counterclockwise. "Deosil" rituals are for banishing, tearing down, endings.

The festival of Light- Christmas- shortest day of the year- was held long before Christ was born.
Winter solstice-Christ's birthday is a Christian event. Christmas associated with Christ being the light of the world-festival of light.
Jehovah's witnesses- don't practice holidays because holidays go back to pagan practices.
Jewish holidays- The Macabee clan went out to keep lights going in the temple-winter solstice.

While there is a Matriarchial system to embrace, there is a Patriarchial insistence to re-define and exclude.

As far back as we know, the Celtic people were the originators of the tree and its connection to the winter solstice.

Druids and Celts were the ones who set up the family crest system in Europe.

The Pagan Creed:
Universal laws:
All things are contained
All things are born of women
Nothing shall be done to harm the children
Cosmic Laws:

1. Death brings life
2. Life brings rebirth
3. Rebirth brings movement
4. As above, so below
5. Movement brings change
6. Change brings chaos
7. Chaos brings death
8. As above, so below

The five Tyrants of life itself:
1. environment
2. time
3. two legged tyrants
4. self
5. situations

In the Pagan system, there are 10 chakras:

First there was the sun
Halo-spirit
Sacred chakras
Above it all
Etheric auric chakra
Body chakra

The seven body elemental kingdoms corresponding to the seven color chakras are:

Crown-1-Dreams, unconscious connection
- Brow-2-Ancestors
- Throat-3-Human
- Heart-4-Animals
- Solar Plexus5-Plants
- Sacral-6-Earth
- Root-7 sun- in the beginning, was the sun

From the top chakra down, each elemental kingdom maintains its evolutionary structure and density. Each kingdom divides down into specific minerals, plants, animals, elemental beings and other things for that chakra.

The Elemental Kingdoms are the halos of wisdom and goodness that circle each chakra, dispersing the compounds of that goodness and wisdom into each and every kind of chakra on the Earth.

The instinctual nature of our consciousness of the elements, of the land and sea, the air and sun, lie rooted deep within each of us.

Our growth is only forwarded by successful interaction with Nature. Attempting to understand Nature on her terms, rather than expecting her to conform to our terms, is the true way this happens.

Almost every custom that is connected to a season goes back a long time ago.

December twenty fourth is the Feast of Adam and Eve throughout Europe. You will find apples everywhere on that day. In Europe and other places, old legends about Evils are traditionally loosed and released during Christmas Eve through New Year's Eve. Pine was, and is still burned to expel the evils.

There is much noisy discord associated with these rituals- witches and evil spirits- said to be in trees-these 12 days of Christmas.

Elemental People and their Values:

Chemicals contain memories. There are different chemicals in the different kinds of tears we cry, and in our laughter.

Men and women hear differently. Pagans know this.

The sense of taste, touch, smell, sight or hearing, can be used as healing tools.

Smell:
The olfactory nerves are brain cells that exist outside of the brain cavity. The olfactory nerves link to the immune system and monitor it through the sense of smell. Odors have a profound effect on our moods, thoughts and emotions. This has been long known and used by spiritual seekers from many cultures.
Olfactory images are recognized by the oldest part of the brain, which is not censored by conscious thought. The specific memories that smells trigger, may even be hereditary. Many rituals involve the use of scents that are derived from ancient temple worship days.

Sweat:
Sweat is considered sacred, and has been collected for use in rituals by Aztecs, Pagans and other groups for centuries.
When we sweat, we exude energies. Liquid from the exhalation of sweat was considered by ancient alchemists to be akin to vapor, which was spiritual. Animals know what condition each other is in by the smell. They know if another animal is sick or in fear. Sweating is one of the body's natural ways of releasing toxins and it is a natural cooling system for the physical body.

People who work with the elements are usually slower and more deliberate than others.

There is an emphasis on the development of the five senses in the elemental kingdoms. Time works differently in the kingdoms than it does here. The more developed the attributes connected to one of the senses becomes, the higher up the status of that nature being or human being. They have earned that development and the honor in the kingdoms that go with it.
Physical attributes of the gaining of elemental wisdom are gifted to persons or passed down through families.
How that development might show up in the physical in an elemental family or in a person, varies. For example, some families may have huge, tiny, or pointed ears.
Each of these physical attributes symbolize different levels of the sense of hearing. Sharp chins, large noses, or big hands or feet denote a higher level of development of one or other of the senses. Sometimes moles, tiny or very large mouths, peculiar kinds of hair, widow's peaks, and other things appear in families.

These accented features or ways, are signs of high honor; gifts from the royalty of the elemental kingdoms. These physical signs all denote a high degree of development of one or more of the five physical senses. That person may have a high status in one of the elemental kingdoms, and has earned the right to wear that physical sign of Status in our world.

Elemental people tend to be heavier and rounder, more solid, and slower and quieter. Elemental body types carry the roots of the Elemental kingdom they are most developed in.

Elementally polarized people think in a circular instead of a linear fashion. Their inner being guides them through life, using their five senses.

Elementally polarized people are living symbols of the ancient root memories we humans carry collectively; they keep the roots of inner stillness and magic each of us carry within ourselves alive. They mirror that for us.

Elementally polarized people assist people to develop character. Attributes come from character development, and are given through the elemental energies. They mirror the living, physical, moral and ethical codes of elemental life.

Elemental people work with the principles of Matter and manifestation of Form. They inject life truths into stories and riddles. They speak in parables and use repetitive mantras with a deeper meaning. They invite us through their magnetism, to participate with them in deliberately searching out wisdom, and to earn the right to know more about the mysteries.

Pay attention and learn when one of these precious people come into your world, for they have no need to change who you are, or who they are, or the kingdoms they are a part of. There are no hidden agendas. They keep the vigil for us and remind us that we are not governed entirely by the outer world we see around us; that there is a world of magic and power within each of us.

Do not succumb to fright or self indulgence.

"There are three centers of what might be called mythological and folkloristic creativity in the Middle Ages. One is the cathedral and all that is associated with monasteries and hermitages. A second is the castle. The third is the cottage. You go to any of the areas of high civilization, and you will see the same; the temple, the palace, and the town. They are different generating centers, but insofar as this is one civilization, they are all operating in the same symbolic field."

Joseph Campbell

Elemental Stories:
Elemental stories remind us of our five senses so that we might engage with more wisdom and learn from them. Each sense provides us with a different kind of understanding of every story we encounter.
A sample of seasonal story themes:

- ϖ Spring- Easter stories, Orphans
- ϖ Summer- Given too much to handle-the Budda
- ϖ Fall-Brer Rabbit- Tricked again, don't ask questions, mommy and daddy
- ϖ Winter-Rip Van Winkle and the Ice Queen

Medieval stories turned counter clockwise, and were passed down in an oral tradition. The stories of modern times began to be told clockwise between the advent of the printing press in the 1500's, and the emergence of the "Romantic" era in the 1600's.

In Medieval stories, all people held ranks or belonged to an "estate", or to a particular group of people.

The highest or part of the group, or First Estate, were the nobility and military ranks. The Second were the peasants and working classes. Third were the clergy and statesmen, followed by trades and industrial.

The stories happened in the:

- ϖ Country
- ϖ City, town, or village
- ϖ Churches or cottages
- ϖ Cemeteries
- ϖ Parsonages
- ϖ Estates
- ϖ Mansions

Most medieval stories are elemental stories because they had to deal with nature in a much more direct way than we have to now. Most elemental stories are about survival skills. They keep a realistic view of life through looking at the negative, the ugly and bold, and the positive capabilities to be gained in the situation.

The study of the Tarot is a method of learning about the Elemental Kingdoms.

To create the circle in the square was the ultimate aim of medieval alchemy.

Elementally polarized stories involve nature, the great outdoors, animals. The seasons are always involved.

- ϖ Example of Books
    - o Narnia books
    - o Dickens
    - o Emily Dickenson
    - o fairy tales
- ϖ Movies
    - o Rambo series
    - o On Golden Pond
    - o Castaway
    - o Horse movies, Black Stallion, The Yearling
    - o The old Tarzan movies
    - o Lassie

Elemental stories are tied to nature and usually take place outdoors in Nature. There is much usage of a particular element, like the sun or rain. This usage indicates the nature and placement of the character development that is taking place in the plot.

Some other things that show up might be:

- o Elders
- o Crones
- o simple objects
- o children
- o old people
- o nature
- o Salamanders
- o Sylphs
- o Caves
- o Bones
- o Mentors
- o Mermaids
- o Undines
- o Gnomes
- o and many more

Elemental Masters and their stories:
It is said that the Christ is the purified mind, and the Buddha is the liberated mind on the elemental planes of energy.
On the physical plane, we have had Master teachers who transmuted, who rose above the laws that govern humankind. All of life desires to participate in this same evolutionary process. Even though they lived thousands of years ago, the principles they lived and taught are still the same principles we live life through today.
These Elemental Master show us that nothing is impossible. They keep humanity's hopes and dreams alive, and our Spirits fed. They are the "glue" that holds the collective mythological energy structures together so that the spiritual future of humanity can be created.

ϖ	Red objects work with the organic understanding of the self.

ϖ	There are older and younger generations that want to know these things.

ϖ	Philosophy and spirit are essential to science for recognizing the patterns of the infinite.

ϖ	Wisdom is the integration between love and will. It manifests as connection in the whole of creation.

We have all of the equipment we need to discover who we are. It is not our destiny to take on someone else's philosophy of life, but to develop our own philosophy of living, to know the truth for our self.

Hands:
Right Hand;
Oh mom-ohm, ahm; these sounds clears atmosphere so you can
see better. Make a circle of thumb and ether finger of right hand.
Elemental placements for balanced energies;

Right thumb;
Air element
Mental body
Gold
Sound- e probing

First finger;
Fire finger
Soul body
silver
2x sound- ahm aim, draw out the m

Second finger
Ether element
Spirit
Unmanifest body
purple
Sound- 2x ahm,aim

Third finger
Earth element
Physical body
indigo
3x om, om,om

Little finger
Water element
Emotional (astral) body
blue
Sound- long oO
Left hand:

A mistake made: harm done: fixed as much as possible: sorrow over what is left. Used to activate sympathetic in support of something that can't be undone.

Thumb;
Color-White
Element- Air
Sound- ng

1st finger
Element-Fire
Color- Red
Sound-long e

Second finger
Element- ether
Color-Orange
Sound- eh.eh, almost yeah

Third finger
Element- Earth
Color- Yellow
Sound-ah at back of throat

Little finger
Element- Water
Color- Green
Sound- long a

Hold hand palm down when using these sounds.

The Highway Men

I was a highway man
Along the coach roads I did ride
With sword and pistol by my side
Many a young maid lost her baubles to my trade
Many a soldier shed his lifeblood on my blade
The bastards hung me in the spring of twenty five
But I am still alive

I was a sailor
I was born upon the tide
And with the sea I did abide
I sailed a schooner around the Horn to Mexico
I went aloft and furled the mainsail in a blow
And when the yards broke off they said that I got killed
But I am living still

I was a dam builder
Across the river deep and wide
Where steel and water did collide
A place called Boulder on the wild Colorado
I slipped and fell into the wet concrete below
But I am still around
I'll always be around and around and around and around and
around

I fly a starship
across the Universe divide
and when I reach the other side
I'll find a place to rest my spirit if I can
Perhaps I will become a highway man again
Or I may be a single drop of rain
But I will remain
And I'll be back again and again and again and again and again.